THIS WALKER BOOK BELONGS TO:

_____

_____

_____

_____

For Barbara, who makes bears
S.H.

For Edward (Teddy) Craig
H.C.

First published 1986 by
Walker Books Ltd
87 Vauxhall Walk
London SE11 5HJ

This edition published 1988

12 14 16 18 20 19 17 15 13 11

Text © 1986 Sarah Hayes
Illustrations © 1986 Helen Craig

Printed in Hong Kong

British Library Cataloguing in Publication Data
A catalogue record for this book is
available from the British Library.
ISBN 0-7445-0969-6

— THIS IS THE —
BEAR

WRITTEN BY
Sarah Hayes

ILLUSTRATED BY
Helen Craig

WALKER BOOKS
AND SUBSIDIARIES
LONDON · BOSTON · SYDNEY

This is the bear
who fell in the bin.

This is the dog
who pushed him in.

This is the man
who picked up the sack.

This is the driver
who would not come back.

This is the bear

who went to the dump

and fell on the pile
with a bit of a bump.

This is the boy

who took the bus

and went to the dump
to make a fuss.

This is the man
in an awful grump
who searched

and searched
and searched the dump.

This is the bear
all cold and cross

who did not think

he was really lost.

This is the dog
who smelled the smell

of a bone

and a tin

and a bear as well.

This is the man

who drove them home –

the boy, the bear
and the dog with a bone.

This is the bear
all lovely and clean

who did not say
just where he had been.

This is the boy
who knew quite well,

but promised his friend

he would not tell.

And this is the boy
who woke up in the night
and asked the bear
if he felt all right –
and was very surprised
when the bear shouted out,
'How soon can we have
another day out?'

MORE WALKER PAPERBACKS
For You to Enjoy

Also by Sarah Hayes and Helen Craig

THIS IS THE BEAR AND THE PICNIC LUNCH
THIS IS THE BEAR AND THE SCARY NIGHT
THIS IS THE BEAR AND THE BAD LITTLE GIRL

Three more great stories about the boy, the dog and the bear.

"Anyone old enough to be attached to a teddy bear will be enchanted…
Sarah Hayes' rhyming couplets work very well, and Helen Craig's
illustrations are just right." *Wendy Cope, The Daily Telegraph*

0-7445-1304-9   *This Is the Bear and the Picnic Lunch*   £4.99
0-7445-3147-0   *This Is the Bear and the Scary Night*   £4.50
0-7445-4771-7   *This Is the Bear and the Bad Little Girl*   £4.99

CRUMBLING CASTLE

Three stories about the wizard Zebulum, his crow assistant
Jason, and their weird and wonderful friends.

"Gentle, cosy magic for solo readers at the lower end of the
junior school who will enjoy Helen Craig's amusing, detailed
line drawings." *Books for Keeps*

0-7445-6082-9   £3.50

MARY MARY

A contrary girl meets and sorts out a ramshackle giant.

"Helen Craig's pictures of the giant are just right." *The Teacher*

0-7445-2062-2   £4.99